NIGHT AT THE MUSEUM
BATTLE OF THE SMITHSONIAN

MADE YOU LOOK!

Adapted by Lucy Rosen
Based on the screenplay
by Robert Ben Garant & Thomas Lennon

HarperEntertainment
An Imprint of HarperCollins Publishers

HarperCollins®, , and HarperEntertainment™ are trademarks of HarperCollins Publishers.

Night at the Museum: Battle of the Smithsonian: Made You Look!
Night at the Museum: Battle of the Smithsonian ™ and © 2009 Twentieth Century Fox Film Corporation.
All Rights Reserved.
Printed in the United States of America.
No part of this book may be used or reproduced in any manner whatsoever without written permission
except in the case of brief quotations embodied in critical articles and reviews. For information address
HarperCollins Children's Books, a division of HarperCollins Publishers, 1350 Avenue of the Americas,
New York, NY 10019.
www.harpercollinschildrens.com

Library of Congress catalog card number: 2008944200
ISBN 978-0-06-171559-4

Typography by Rick Farley and John Sazaklis
❖
First Edition

Are you ready for some fun?
The picture pairs in this book may seem the same,
but look closely—they're not! What's different?
Are there things missing?

Can you find all of the differences?

MADE YOU LOOK!

When Pharaohs Attack!
Kahmunrah has Larry cornered.

D0521259

Monkeying Around
Able is a sneaky little fellow.

BALE

Searching High and Low
Amelia looks everywhere for the Golden Tablet!

Crash Landing!
Larry races his motorcycle while trying to escape danger.

Mafia Mayhem

Al Capone and his pals mean business.

Free to Be Dr. McPhee

Dr. McPhee looks a little different in the picture on the right.

Thank You for Flying Air Earhart!

Amelia Earhart has landed her plane outside of the museum.

Gone from the Gallery
The Smithsonian is full of beautiful art.

Hey There, Little Fella!

Napoleon takes Larry to his leader.

Wright Brothers, Wrong Picture
Mmm! Ice Cream!

Mob in an Elevator
They're going down!

There's a Monkey with My Tablet!
Able snatches the Golden Tablet away from Larry.

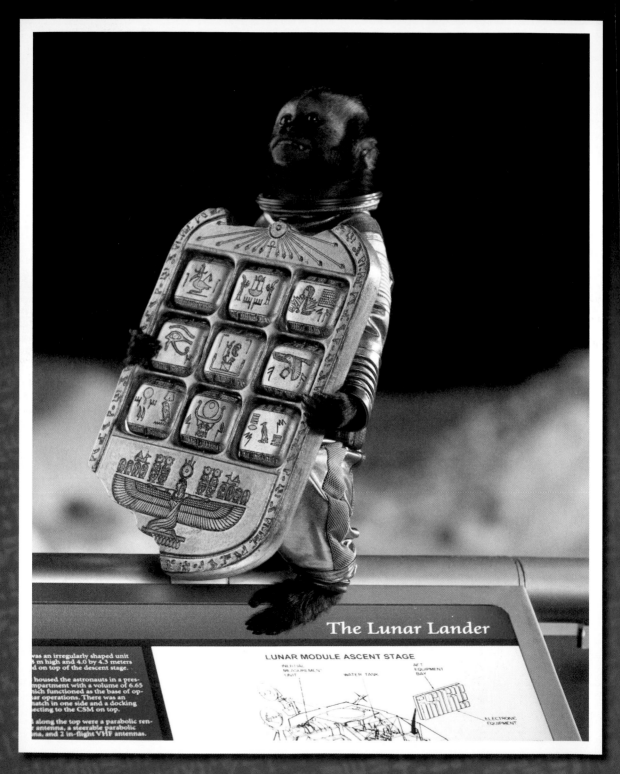

The Lunar Lander

LUNAR MODULE ASCENT STAGE

...was an irregularly shaped unit
...8 m high and 4.0 by 4.3 meters
...d on top of the descent stage.

...housed the astronauts in a pres-
...mpartment with a volume of 6.65
...hich functioned as the base of op-
...r operations. There was an
...atch in one side and a docking
...ecting to the CSM on top.

...along the top were a parabolic ren-
...r antenna, a steerable parabolic
...na, and 2 in-flight VHF antennas.

was an irregularly shaped unit
8 m high and 4.0 by 4.3 meters
d on top of the descent stage.

housed the astronauts in a pres-
mpartment with a volume of 6.65
hich functioned as the base of op-
ar operations. There was an
hatch in one side and a docking
ecting to the CSM on top.

along the top were a parabolic ren-
r antenna, a steerable parabolic
na, and 2 in-flight VHF antennas.

LUNAR MODULE ASCENT STAGE

INERTIAL
MEASUREMENT
UNIT

WATER TANK

AFT
EQUIPMENT
BAY

ELECTRONIC
EQUIPMENT

Ready, Set, Charge!

Amelia leads the way to join in the fight against Kahmunrah.

The Air and Space Museum

Mission control, we have a problem.

Custer's Surprise

General Custer is ready to fight for his friends!

Evil Comes in Threes
Ivan, Al Capone, and Napoleon don't give up very easily.

Kahmunrah Cashes In

The evil pharaoh collects treasures from all over the museum.

Rexy Rears His Head

The gang is back in New York at last, and Rexy couldn't be happier!

ANSWERS

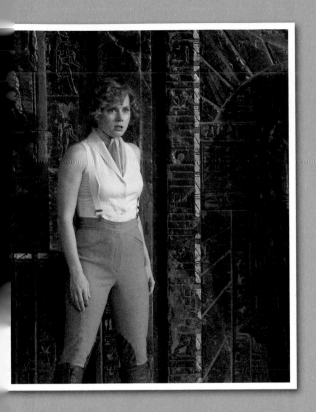

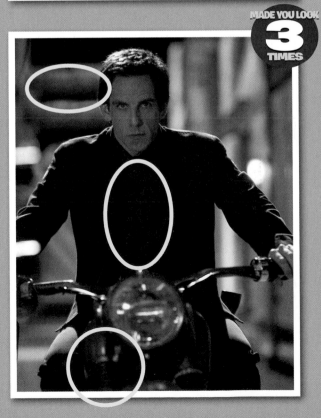

ANSWERS

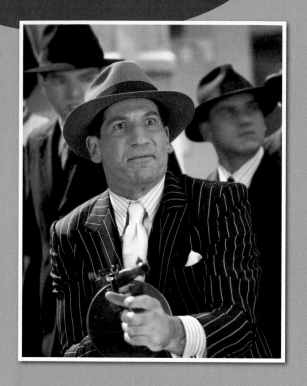

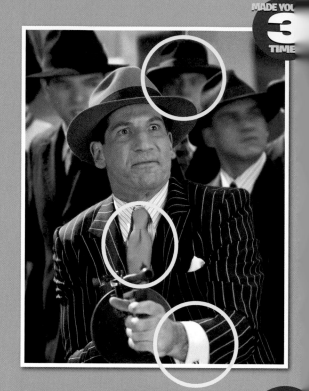

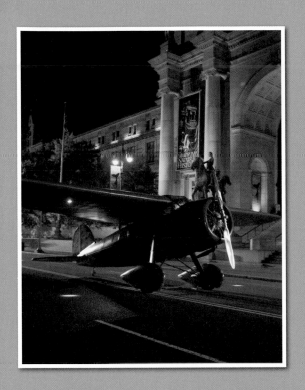

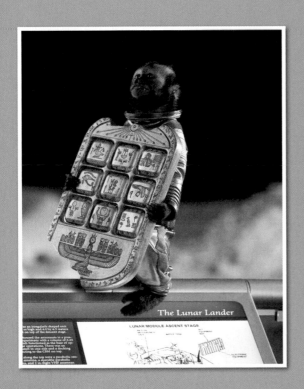

The Lunar Lander

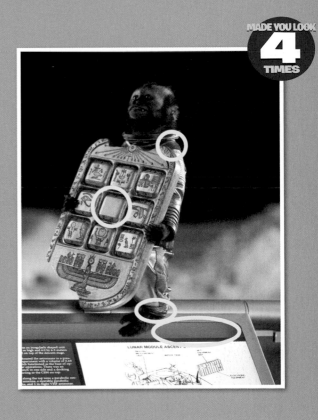

ANSWERS

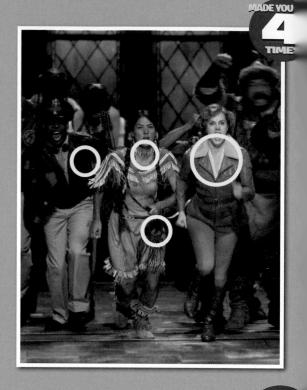

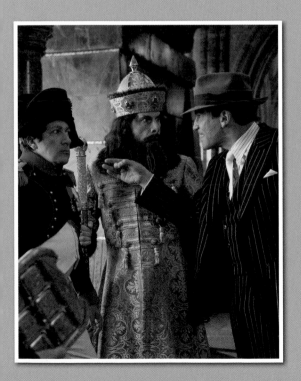

ANSWERS